and the

HALLOWEEN

scream

MONICA BROWN

LOLA LEVINE

and the

HALLOWEEN

Scream

ILLUSTRATED BY
Angela Dominguez

LITTLE, BROWN AND COMPANY
New York • Boston

Text copyright © 2017 by Monica Brown
Interior Artwork copyright © 2017 by Angela Dominguez
Pumpkins by Tatiana, SK

Cover design by Marcie Lawrence. Cover art copyright © 2017 by Angela Dominguez. Cover copyright © 2017 by Hachette Book Group, Inc.

Little, Brown and Company
Hachette Book Group
1290 Avenue of the Americas, New York, NY 10104
Visit us at lb-kids.com

First Edition: July 2017

Little, Brown and Company is a division of Hachette Book Group, Inc.
The Little, Brown name and logo are trademarks of Hachette Book Group, Inc.

The publisher is not responsible for websites (or their content) that are not owned by the publisher.

ISBNs: 978-0-316-50642-7 (hardcover), 978-0-316-50643-4 (pbk.), 978-0-316-50640-3 (ebook)

Printed in the United States of America

LSC-C

10 9 8 7 6 5 4 3 2 1

To Nikki Garcia, with joy and gratitude

CONTENTS

Chapter One

Boo!.....3

Chapter Two

Leaf Art.....15

Chapter Three

Zombies and Llamas.....25

Chapter Four

Apples and Pumpkins.....35

Chapter Five

The Parade.....49

Chapter Six

Trick.....57

Chapter Seven

Treat.....71

Chapter Eight

Strong Bodies.....81

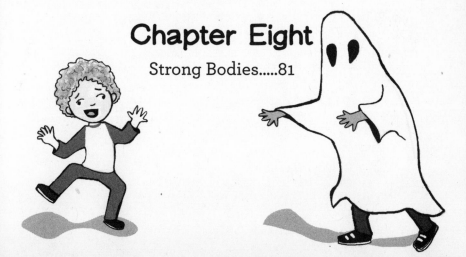

Dear *Diario*,

Yay! It's almost Halloween! And
since Halloween is on a Sunday
this year, it's going to be a
Halloweekend! I am so excited.
Halloween is one of my favorite
holidays, and not just because
I love witches and ghosts and
monsters, but also because I love
candy! And I really don't get to
eat a lot of candy, except for
Halloween. My parents don't let
me. Mom says that candy doesn't
help build strong bodies. When
we want something sweet, she
sometimes suggests raisins, which
she says are "nature's candy."

1

About two days after Halloween,
Mom always has the idea that we
should trade what's left of our
candy for something else, like a
new book or toy. It's her idea,
not ours, but it seems like we
always end up agreeing to Mom's
ideas. I'm getting sleepy now, so...

Shalom and good night,
Lola Levine

Chapter One
Boo!

On Monday morning, I wake up extra early because I have a plan. My plan is to scare my little brother, Ben. He's okay most of the time, but he also bugs me. He likes to make jokes, and sometimes they are about me.

Last week, he kept saying "Dolores is a brontosaurus! Dolores is a brontosaurus!" because he likes rhymes. Dolores is my first name, but I go by Lola.

"I'm NOT a brontosaurus!" I tell Ben. "Dinosaurs have small brains, and mine is big!"

Ben might be good at rhyming, but guess what? I'm good at scaring people, and since it's almost Halloween, I'm going to scare Ben this morning. I wait outside his door until I hear my dad call up the stairs like he does every morning before school.

"Kids! Wake up! Breakfast in fifteen minutes!"

I hear some mumbles and grumbles, and then I hear Ben get up. I know he'll come out of his room soon, so I pretend to be a ghost and throw on a white sheet with holes cut out for the eyes. I crouch and wait, and when Ben steps into the hallway, I jump out in front of him and say, "Boo!" Ben jumps back and trips over his own feet. "Gotcha!" I say, and start laughing.

Ben does not think this is as funny as I do.

"You scared me, Lola! And it's not even Halloween yet," he complains.

"Well, it's Halloweek," I say, and pat him on the head. Then I go back to my room to get ready for school.

"I'll get you back!" Ben says.

"I hope so!" I say. I like surprises.

Dad makes us pumpkin pancakes for breakfast. Not only do they have pumpkin flavor, but they are shaped like pumpkins, too! It's going to be a great day.

When I get to school, I run over to Josh Blot and Bella Benitez, my super best friends.

"What are you going to be for Halloween?" I ask.

"I'm going to be a firefighter," says Josh.

"That's awesome," I say. "How about you, Bella?"

"I'm going to be a fairy," she says.

"How cool!" I say. "You'll be a great fairy. When you dance ballet, it sometimes looks like you are flying." Bella loves to dance.

"How about you?" Bella asks.

"I'm not sure yet," I say. "I might be a zombie—or a vampire. It has to be something really scary. We always make our costumes, because my dad believes in 'creative expression,' but we did buy lots of black and white makeup and fake blood at the store this weekend."

Alyssa Goldstein and Makayla Miller must be listening, because all of a sudden Alyssa says, "Gross. I don't know why you'd want to wear fake blood or look like a monster."

"I happen to like monsters," I say back. "What are you going to be for Halloween?"

"Princesses," Alyssa and Makayla say at the same time. Somehow, I'm not surprised. They sometimes act like they rule the school, but they really don't. They like to tease me, and other people, too. The bell rings, and we all walk into Ms. Garcia's second-grade classroom and sit down.

"Good morning, students!" Ms. Garcia says.

"Good morning, Ms. Garcia!" we answer back.

"Is everyone excited for the Fall Festival?" Ms. Garcia asks.

"Yes!" the whole class says at once.

"We are going to have so many fun events this week," Ms. Garcia says. "There are lots of celebrations during the fall,

all over the world. For example, Chinese people celebrate the Moon Festival in mid-autumn. They gather with friends and family for parades under the moonlight, carrying lanterns and dancing. They celebrate, give thanks, and eat mooncakes.

"Mexicans and Mexican Americans like me celebrate Dia de los Muertos, the Day of the Dead, at the start of November. We create altars for our loved ones who have passed. Many in the United States celebrate Halloween."

"We celebrate Dia de los Muertos, too!" says Bella.

"That's wonderful!" says Ms. Garcia. "Fall is an important time of year for many people. Here at Northland Elementary we will have the Fall Festival this week to celebrate the transition of summer into winter during the season of autumn."

"I know a girl named Autumn!" says Juan Gomez. "She lives on my block."

"That's a nice name," says Ms. Garcia. "What do we know about autumn, the season also called fall?" I raise my hand, and Ms. Garcia calls on me.

"It's the time of year when trees' leaves change color and then fall off," I say.

"That's right, Lola," says Ms. Garcia. "We have four seasons: summer, fall, winter, and spring. We call trees that lose all their leaves seasonally deciduous trees." Then she writes the word *deciduous* on the board. It sounds like dee-sid-you-us. "Autumn is also the time when some of the food we eat is harvested, including apples."

"Yum!" I say. "Do we get to visit an apple orchard, Ms. Garcia? Because I know last year's second graders did."

"Yes, we do," says Ms. Garcia. "On Wednesday, we will go to Feliz Manzana Farm and pick some apples. Can anyone tell me what *feliz manzana* means in English?" I raise my hand, but Bella is quicker. "What does it mean, Bella?"

"It means 'happy apple,'" Bella says with a smile.

"I speak Spanish, too," I say.

"We all know that," says Makayla, rolling her eyes. I roll mine back.

"Tomorrow, we'll collect leaves and decorate the classroom with leaf art. We'll visit the farm on Wednesday, and Thursday is Pumpkin Day! Each of you will bring a pumpkin to school. We'll weigh, measure, and describe the pumpkins. After that, you'll get to paint them. And then, finally, we are going to have a school parade on Friday during lunchtime recess. Each of you will get to dress as one of your favorite characters from a book or from history."

I already know who my favorite book character is. I'm going to dress up as Marisol McDonald from my favorite picture book, *Marisol McDonald Doesn't Match*. Marisol is bilingual, just like me. She likes to mismatch on purpose. Best of all, she's always true to herself, even if it means people tease her sometimes.

"Hooray! Hooray! Pumpkin Day!" I say, and everyone laughs. It feels nice— not like they are laughing at me, but like they are laughing with me.

Chapter Two
Leaf Art

When I come home from soccer prac-
tice, I can smell my mom's Peruvian
chicken—yum.

Mom calls us to the table, and as I sit
down for dinner, I notice a rubber spider

on my plate. It's ugly and rubbery, and it doesn't fool me for one minute.

"Nice try, Ben," I say. "This isn't scary at all." He just sticks his tongue out at me.

"I have the best idea in the whole wide world!" he tells us.

"Really?" I ask. "I don't believe you."

"Lola," Mom says, "listen to what your brother has to say."

"Well," says Ben, "you know how we have a Fall Festival parade at school?"

"Of course I know," I say. "We get to dress up as a book character or a historical figure."

"My idea is that we have a pet parade, too!"

"At the same time?" I ask Ben.

"Yes!" he says.

"It's during lunch, right? I was planning on coming," says Mom. "I could always stop by the house and pick up Bean."

"That's actually a great idea, Ben. I love it!" I say, giving him a high five.

After dinner, I help Ben write a letter.

Dear Principal Blot,

My mom says it's good to try new things. So when we have our parade on Friday at lunch recess, I think we should have animals, too! Parents could bring their pets. In costumes! Mom says the pets would be on leashes.

Why? Because pets make people happy!

Please.

From,
Ben Levine

P.S. I helped.

—Lola Levine

After we finish morning lessons the next day, Ms. Garcia asks us the question we've been waiting for. "Are you ready to go on a leaf walk?"

"Yes!" we say.

"Then it's time to bundle up," she says. We are so excited. We hold hands and walk in two lines toward a park near school.

I like the way the leaves sound when they crunch beneath our feet. When we get to the park, Ms. Garcia gives us each a plastic bag and lets us go leaf hunting in pairs. I'm with Josh. We are about to start collecting when I notice something.

"Look, Josh!" I say, and point to several big piles of leaves at the edge of the grass.

I'm about to tell Josh that we should go jump in them when Ms. Garcia says loudly, "One more thing, students! Don't jump in or climb on the piles of leaves because someone worked hard to rake them up." I frown. Sometimes it seems like Ms. Garcia can read my mind. She and my mom have the same superpower, I think!

"But it sounds fun to jump in the leaves," I whisper to myself. It feels like the pile of leaves *wants* me to jump on top of it. But I don't want to get in trouble, so I walk away from the piles and start looking for pretty leaves on the ground. When I find ones I like, I put them into my bag.

When we get back to the classroom, we get a leaf lesson from Ms. Garcia. We learn the different types of trees our leaves came from and write descriptions of each tree. We glue a leaf of each kind and color onto a page in a book Ms. Garcia calls *The Northland Elementary Big Book of Leaves.* Then the super-fun part. We get to make leaf art animals! Ms. Garcia gets out paper, glue sticks, and little googly eyes that can stick on the leaves.

"I'm going to make an owl!" says Josh.

"I think I'll make a fox," says Bella.

"Let's make fish!" Alyssa tells Makayla.

"Hmmm," says Makayla. "I think I'd rather make a turkey."

"Fine," says Alyssa, scowling. I don't think she likes it when people don't do what she wants.

I can't decide what to make. I raise my hand.

"Can I make a leaf monster?" I ask Ms. Garcia.

"For this assignment, I'd like you to think creatively about an animal you can make from leaves, Lola," Ms. Garcia says.

"Can my animal be scary?" I ask.

"Sure," Ms. Garcia says. At first, I think I'll make a lion because lions have loud roars, but then I think of something even better.

"I'll make a mouse!" I say. "Lots of people scream when they see mice."

"Why do you like to hear people scream?" asks Bella.

"Because it's fun to scare people—isn't it?" I ask.

"I don't think so," says Bella. Maybe she doesn't like mice.

"You are SO weird," says Alyssa, gluing a googly eye on her fish.

After school, I invite Josh, Juan, and Bella to trick-or-treat with me on Halloween.

"You can bring your parents, too," I say.

"I know I'll be able to come!" says Josh.

We've been trick-or-treating together since we were little.

"I'll ask my parents," says Bella. "That sounds like fun!"

"I usually go with my cousins, so I don't think I can," says Juan.

"That's okay," I say to Juan. Then I turn to Josh and Bella. "Let's meet at my house early. We can have hot chocolate." I can't wait until Halloween.

Chapter Three
Zombies and Llamas

While Ben and I set the table for dinner, he tells me one Halloween joke after another. He and his friends love jokes. Ben learns a lot of his jokes from his friends, from books, and, secretly, I think, from Dad.

"What do birds say at Halloween?" he asks.

"I don't know, Ben," I say. "What?"

"Trick or tweet!" he says. "And I have another one!"

"Okay, Ben," I say, "just one more."

"Why didn't the skeleton go to the party?" Ben asks, and before I even have a chance to answer, he says, "Because he had no BODY to go with!" I just laugh.

After dinner, Ben and I brainstorm costume ideas with Mom and Dad.

"I could be a zombie," I say. "We could

paint my face white with black under my eyes and rip up some old clothes."

"And we could rub dirt on them so it looks like you used to live below the ground," Dad says.

"And I could walk like this!" I say, sticking my arms and legs straight out in front of me.

"I can walk that way, too!" Ben says, jumping up and following me around the living room.

"What do you want to be for Halloween, Ben?" asks Mom.

"Mira and I decided to be a wolf and a lamb," he says. Mira Goldstein is Ben's best friend. She's so nice that I can hardly believe her older sister is Alyssa.

"That's cool! You'll be the wolf," I say, and start walking on all fours.

"Actually, I'm going to be the lamb," Ben says. "That's okay, right?"

"Of course it is!" Mom says.

"Mira is going to be the wolf that chases me," Ben says.

"It will be a fun costume to make, Ben—we'll use lots of cotton balls," says Dad.

"You're going to be a lamb?" I say. "The one that gets scared?"

"What's wrong with that?" Mom asks. "When we dress up in costumes, we are playing pretend. It's not real."

"I know," I say, "but it's Halloween! Don't you want to be scary?"

"We all get to choose how to celebrate

Halloween," Dad says. "If Ben wants to be a lamb, then that's his choice."

"We are all unique, and we sometimes like different things," Mom says. "If we were exactly the same, it would be pretty boring." I get it.

"Ben, you are going to be one cute lamb," I say, and my dad smiles.

"Well," Dad says, "we've got a lamb and a zombie for Halloween trick-or-treating."

"Now, what about the Fall Festival parade?" asks Mom. "I know Lola is going as Marisol McDonald. Have you thought about a book character, Ben?"

"Not yet," he says.

"Well, what are your favorite books?" I ask.

"I have lots of favorites!" he says.

"What book did you have me read last night, and the night before that, Ben?" Dad asks.

"*Maria Had a Little Llama!*" Ben answers. Ever since we got back from visiting our *tía* Lola in Peru, Ben has been obsessed with llamas. He even has a stuffed llama named Lorenzo that he carries around everywhere.

"You know, Ben," I say, "you can be Maria *or* the llama." This time I want to make sure he knows he can be whatever he wants to be.

"I want to be a llama!" he says. "Can we do that, Dad?"

"Of course!" says Dad.

"Maybe you can use cardboard," Mom says.

"Yay!" says Ben. "I'm going to be a llama, Mama!"

"And we can dress Bean up like Maria!" I say.

"Yes!" says Ben, jumping up and down. "Bean will dress up for Halloween! He'll be our Halloween Bean!" My brother sure does like to rhyme.

Mom and Dad decide that I should go to bed early, because of the field trip to Feliz Manzana Farm tomorrow. The problem is, talking about costumes made me so excited that I'm not even one bit sleepy! I decide to write in my diary.

Dear *Diario,*

Today I made a mouse out of leaves! I also went on a leaf walk and did some leaf collecting. I wanted to do some leaf jumping and throwing, but I didn't. And I still had a lot of fun. I'm really, really excited to be a zombie. Do zombie's talk? I wonder. Or do I just have to grunt? Since zombies

are make-believe, I can be any
kind of zombie I want. But a
talking zombie doesn't sound very
scary.

Shalom,
Lola Levine

Chapter Four
Apples and Pumpkins

Today when Dad drives us to school, he doesn't just drop Ben and me off—he parks the car and gets out. He is a parent chaperone on our field trip. Because my dad works in his art studio at home, he can make his own schedule. My mom works all day at the newspaper. She even has to go in at night sometimes.

We drive to the farm in a big yellow school bus. Dad rides in the front with Ms. Garcia and some other parents. The drive takes such a long time! I am happy when we get out and I can stretch my legs. A lady dressed in overalls and boots greets us. She has a big smile on her face.

"Welcome, Northland students," she says. "I'm Ms. Carolyn, and this is my family's farm. We are going to have fun this morning!" Ms. Carolyn leads us on a walk to the orchard, where Ms. Garcia breaks us up into teams of four or five. Each team gets to fill a basket with apples.

"There are only a few rules," Ms. Carolyn says. "First, I want to show you how to pick an apple." She uses one hand to hold the branch and the other hand to slowly twist the apple until it comes off.

"Don't pull," Ms. Carolyn says, "or the branch will shake and apples will fall and bruise. Also, don't eat the apples until you have a chance to wash them at home. Oh, and one more thing—no climbing on the trees." I don't know why, but my dad looks straight at me just then and raises his eyebrows at me.

We then walk a little farther to the part of the farm where the apples are ready to be picked. All of a sudden, Bella grabs my hand.

"Look!" she says. She points to what looks like a person up high on a wooden pole.

"It's a scarecrow!" I say, smiling. "It scares away birds, I think."

"Ms. Carolyn!" Bella raises her hand. "Why would anyone want to scare away birds? Birds are nice."

"Birds are delightful, but they sometimes eat seeds and young crops. That's why you find scarecrows on many farms," Ms. Carolyn says.

"Maybe I'll be a scarecrow for Halloween," I say. "What's scarier than a scarecrow?!"

"They give me goose bumps," Bella says. I pick up some straw from the ground and tickle Bella with it.

"The scarecrow is coming to get you," I say, laughing.

"That's not funny!" Bella says.

"But scarecrows aren't real," I say.

"They're real enough to me. Stop trying to scare me!" she says, and then she stomps away and joins a different group for apple picking. I didn't realize ballerinas were such good stompers.

Apple picking isn't nearly as fun without Bella, but at least I'm in the same group as Josh, Juan, and my dad. After we finish picking apples, we get to taste some apple cider made fresh on the farm. I love it, and Dad buys some to bring home and share with my mom and Ben. When I get back on the bus, I walk toward Bella. She's already seated.

"Can I sit here?" I ask.

"Okay," says Bella, "but I still don't like scarecrows."

"What do you like?" I ask Bella.

"Bunnies! And fairies. And butterflies and unicorns," Bella says.

"Unicorns are pretty cool," I agree.

The next day, I wake up and write a note—but not in my *diario*. This time, I'm writing to Principal Blot.

Dear Principal Blot,

It's Lola. My brother doesn't know I'm writing you. Please don't tell him. Have you had enough time

to decide if we can bring our
pets to the Fall Festival parade?
Because it's tomorrow! I hope
you have, and I hope the answer
is yes. Ben is very excited about
this. Even though he bugs me
sometimes, I don't want him to be
disappointed.

Shalom,
Lola Levine

When I get to school, I stop by the
front office. I see Principal Blot sitting at
her desk.

"Hi, Principal Blot!" I say loudly. "Can
I see you for a second?" Principal Blot
waves me in.

"What's the problem, Lola?" she asks.

"There's no problem," I say. "I know I'm usually in trouble when I'm in your office, but not today. I'm just here to give you a note. About having pets at the Fall Festival parade."

"Okay, Lola. You may leave it on my desk," she says, and I do.

"How are Milo and Jelly?" I ask, because I want to remind her that she has pets that she loves very much.

"They are fine," she says. "Shouldn't you be going, Lola?"

"Why?" I ask.

"Because the bell just rang and you are now late for class," she says. "Here's a tardy slip."

"Have a super great day, Principal

Blot!" I say as I leave. "Don't forget to read my note!"

"I won't," Principal Blot says.

When it's time to paint our pumpkins, I bring mine over to where Bella is sitting.

"Are you going to paint a bunny face on your pumpkin?" I ask Bella.

"No," she says, and smiles. "I'm going to paint a happy pumpkin in all my favorite colors." As far as I know, Bella's only favorite color is pink. She wears something pink almost every day.

"I'll use light pink, dark pink, ballerina pink, magenta, purply-pink, and pinkish-purple," she says, and I smile.

"I'm going to paint my pumpkin all black and then make white designs on it," I say, and Bella laughs. I look over and see Josh and Juan making their pumpkins into soccer balls. Why didn't I think of that?

"I love your pumpkins!" I tell them. "Will your soccer pumpkins have faces?"

"Of course!" says Josh.

We are in the middle of pumpkin painting when we hear a ding from the speaker above the door. This means an announcement is coming.

"ATTENTION, NORTHLAND ELE-MENTARY STUDENTS," a loud voice says. "THIS IS PRINCIPAL BLOT, AND I HAVE A SPECIAL ANNOUNCEMENT. WE WILL BE SENDING A NOTE HOME

TO YOUR PARENTS, BUT I WANTED YOU TO KNOW THAT THIS YEAR, WE WILL BE ALLOWING PETS ON CAM- PUS DURING THE FALL FESTIVAL PARADE—FROM NOON TO ONE PM ONLY, AND THEY MUST BE WITH YOUR PARENTS AND ON A LEASH. PET COSTUMES ARE OKAY, TOO, BUT THE SAME RULES APPLY— HISTORICAL FIGURES OR BOOK CHARACTERS. HAVE A NICE AFTER- NOON."

Then we hear another ding, and things are silent, but only for a second. Then everyone is clapping and saying "Yay!" I'm happy for myself, but I'm even happier for Ben. I swear I can hear his "Whoopee!" from two classrooms away.

Dear *Diario,*

Tomorrow is the Fall Festival parade. Yay! Ben is so excited to dress up Bean. I'm excited, too. I wonder if Principal Blot will wear a costume. I hope so!

Shalom,
Lola Levine

Chapter Five
The Parade

On Friday morning, I wake up to the sound of a big crash. "Mom! Dad?" I say really loudly, but no one answers. Then I hear Ben's voice right outside my bedroom door.

"Help, Lola! Help!" Oh no, I think, what has he gotten into now? I jump out of bed and run into Ben's room. Ben is lying on the floor moaning, and it looks like the bookshelf has fallen on top of him.

"My hand! My hand!" he says, and holds up his hand. His fingers are covered in blood.

"Mom! Dad!" I yell. "Where are you?" I kneel down next to Ben, and then I smell it. Ketchup. *Gross.*

"Ben!" I say. "You got me!"

"I did! I did!" he says, laughing. Mom and Dad jump out from the stairwell and say "Boo!" and we all laugh. They were in on the joke, too.

"Good one, Ben!" I say.

"Now let's go eat breakfast, and then you

can get into your book character costumes. You don't want to be late today!" Dad says.

"It's Friday! It's Parade Day!" says Ben.

"I'm so excited to see you at lunch," I tell Mom.

"I can't wait," she replies, giving me a hug.

"Is Bean's costume ready?" asks Ben.

"It sure is," says Dad.

The first person I see when I get to school is none other than Principal Blot. She's dressed in a long, old-fashioned kind of dress and her hair is in a bun. I run up to her.

"Who are you supposed to be, Principal Blot?" I ask.

"I'm Susan B. Anthony," she says. "She was born almost two hundred years ago, and she fought for women to have the right to vote."

"Wow!" I say. "She made the world a better place."

"She did," Principal Blot says.

"I like your hair that way," I tell Principal Blot.

"Thank you," she says. "I like your costume, Marisol McDonald."

"Thank you back!" I say, then run to get in line outside Ms. Garcia's room.

Bella looks so cool. She has on a colorful skirt and several shawls. Her hair is braided and woven with flowers. She's carrying a paintbrush and a stuffed monkey.

"I'm Frida Kahlo," she explains. "She is

a famous Mexican artist, and she had a pet monkey. I've been to her house in Mexico."

"I'm going to tell my dad you're an artist!" I say. "I bet he knows who Frida is." Josh is dressed as Harry Potter, which isn't a surprise, and Makayla and Alyssa are dressed as Thing One and Thing Two from Dr. Seuss, which *is* a surprise. I guess they

like things other than just princesses. They even have blue hair! I'm mismatched and marvelous like Marisol McDonald, and I'm wearing my Peruvian *chullo* hat, just like her. Juan's dressed up in yellow overalls.

"I'm Thunder Boy!" he tells me.

The parade is super fun. Everyone is dressed up, and there are parents and pets everywhere—mostly dogs, though Alyssa and Mira's mom brought their bunny in a cage. It even has a superhero cape on! Mira is dressed as Little Red Riding Hood, which is funny because I know she's going to be a wolf for Halloween. As soon as I see my mom and Bean arrive, I run up to them and give them both hugs. I ask Ms. Garcia if I can walk with the kindergartners during the parade so I can be with my family, and she says yes.

"You make a great llama!" I tell Ben.

"And Bean makes a great Maria," he says proudly. Bean is definitely excited to be at Northland Elementary, and he makes lots of new friends.

Chapter Six
Trick

At the end of the day, I am a little sad that Halloweek is over at school. At least Halloween is the day after tomorrow. But I want to play one more trick.

I decide to surprise my friends after

school. I put my pumpkin and my back-pack on the ground behind a tree, and then I hide, too. I wait until I see Bella and Josh walking toward the bus stop. Sometimes Josh takes the bus home from school so he doesn't have to wait until his mom is done working. Bella and Josh are carrying their pumpkins and backpacks, and they must be talking about some-thing really funny because they are both laughing. I jump out from behind the tree with my hands in front of me like a zom-bie and yell, "Boo!"

Bella and Josh fall back and some-thing awful happens. Josh drops his pumpkin, and it goes splat on the cement.

"Lola!" Bella says.

"My pumpkin!" says Josh. "It's ruined."

"Oh no!" I say. "I'm so sorry. It was a joke."

"Not to me!" Josh says, trying to put his pumpkin back together.

"You know I don't like being scared," Bella says, "but you did it anyway!"

"I thought it would be funny," I say, but Josh looks like he's about to cry, not laugh. "I'm so sorry."

"Stop saying sorry," Josh says. "I wanted to put my pumpkin in the window to show trick-or-treaters, and now I can't."

"Maybe we can fix it," I say, trying to help.

"Just go away," Josh says, for the first time ever. So I do.

By the time my dad picks me up, I'm crying. Ben is worried because I don't cry very often.

"What's wrong?" Dad asks as I get into the front seat and put on my seat belt. Ben climbs into the back and shuts the door, and I spill out the whole story—about the scarecrow, the smashed pumpkins, and the fact that my two super best friends are *super* mad at me.

"That is a bummer," Dad says. "I can see why you are feeling sad and sorry. Why did you decide to scare them, Lola?"

"Because I thought it would be fun," I answer.

"For who? For them?" Dad asks. I think about it for a little bit.

"No, I thought it would be fun for me," I say. "I know Bella doesn't really like being scared."

"That was a mean thing to do, Lola," Ben says from the backseat.

"It's not your job to tell me that!" I say to Ben. But then I think about it.

"I guess it was a little mean, but I just wanted to have fun."

"Everyone has fun in different ways," Dad says. "We need to listen to our friends."

That night, I can't sleep. I toss and turn and flip my pillow over again and again, but it doesn't work. I try to think of puppies and soccer games, but even that doesn't work. I get out of bed and decide to write in my diary.

Dear *Diario*,

I can't sleep. It's like I've got monkeys jumping up and down in my head, and they are all saying, "You're mean, Lola Levine!" I want to be nice to my friends. I just don't understand why they don't like Halloween jokes as much as me. But if I think about it really hard, maybe I do understand. I always say I like being scared, but

I'm not telling the truth, because right now I feel scared that I might have lost my two best friends.

I think I'm going to go and wake up Mom, because some worries are too big for just one person.

Shalom,
Lola Levine

I peek into my parents' room, and Mom is still awake reading.

"Mom?" I whisper, because I don't want to wake up my dad.

"Hi, sweetie," Mom whispers. "What's wrong?"

"I can't sleep," I tell her, "and I really want to. For real." Mom gets out of bed and gives me a hug.

"Let's go downstairs and have some hot milk," Mom says.

I watch my mom stir the milk in the pot and add a few drops of honey. When it's ready, we take our mugs into the family room, where Bean is happy to see me. Mom and I sit on the couch, and she wraps us in my favorite blanket, the one Grandma Levine, my *bubbe*, knitted for us.

"What are you thinking about, Lola?" Mom asks.

"I'm thinking that Josh and Bella are mad at me," I say. "And I'm thinking that maybe I'm not nice."

"Lola," my mom says, "you are nice.

You're my sunshine girl. I'll tell you what you are not, though...."

"What?" I ask Mom.

"You're not perfect," Mom says. "Nobody is. We all make mistakes, and it's hard to be perfect every second of every day. All we can do is keep trying to be our best selves."

"I'm glad I don't have to be perfect, but I still don't like feeling this way," I tell Mom. "And what am I supposed to do about Josh and Bella?"

"Well, you've said sorry, so the other most important thing is to change your actions."

"You mean I should stop scaring them?" I ask.

"That seems like a good idea, but don't

worry, we can still celebrate the scary parts of Halloween together," Mom says. "Okay?"

"Okay," I say, and I feel better. I always feel better after I talk with Mom. "I don't have to be perfect," I say, "and even if I wanted to, nobody is perfect. I think I can go to sleep now." Mom gives me one more hug and then walks me upstairs and tucks me in.

"I love you, Lola," she says.

"I love you, too, Mom," I say with a yawn.

In the morning, I feel better, and I have a plan. I ask Dad if we can go to the grocery store after breakfast. I bring all the money

I have in my piggy bank and some markers. I buy two pumpkins—a big one to give to Josh so he'll have something to paint today and a little pumpkin for Bella. Dad drives me to Josh's house and I knock on his door. He answers and I give him his pumpkin.

"I'm so sorry," I tell Josh. "I wanted to make sure you had a pumpkin to paint."

"Thanks, Lola," Josh says. "I wasn't really scared, you know. I was more surprised."

"I know," I say, "but I realize it wasn't a very nice thing to do. Most people don't like to be scared or surprised. Will you still come trick-or-treating with me tomorrow?"

"Of course," he says. "I'm going to be a firefighter, remember?"

I'm so relieved. I say good-bye to Josh, and then Dad and I go to Bella's house. No one answers the door. I remember that Bella has ballet on Saturday mornings, so I leave the pumpkin in Bella's mail-box. It's not just a regular pumpkin. It's a pumpkin-gram.

Dear Bella,

I am sorry I didn't listen to your words and scared you again. You are one of my super best friends, and I hope you forgive me.

Shalom,
Lola Levine

I hope Bella forgives me. I'm not sure, though, because I don't hear from her the rest of the day.

Chapter Seven

Treat

Dear *Diario*,

I learned a lot this week. First of
all, some people don't really want a
trick when they say trick or treat.

They just want a treat. I thought hiding behind a tree to scare Josh and Bella would be funny. It wasn't. I learned that if people say they don't like to be scared, I should believe them. But I'm not going to feel bad anymore. I'm not perfect, but I'm not mean, either. I'm just going to try harder to be a good friend. If there's one thing I'm good at, it's trying hard at whatever I do.

Shalom,
Lola Levine

On Sunday morning, I make an announcement. "I don't want to be a zombie for Halloween," I tell my family.

We are in the backyard. I am throwing a ball to Bean, Ben is juggling a soccer ball, and Mom is watering plants. Dad is raking the leaves.

"Why not?" Dad asks.

"I hope it isn't because of what happened with Josh and Bella," Mom says. "Because you still get to be you, Lola. And I know you like to be scary."

"I know," I tell Mom. "I'm just going to try something different this year."

"It sounds like you know what you want to do," says Dad.

"What's your new costume, Lola?" asks Ben.

"Well," I say, "I thought it would be fun if I went dressed as Bean and he went dressed as me!"

"That's an awesome idea, Lola!" Dad says. "We still have some fur from last year when you were a werewolf."

"And we can make a costume for Bean out of one of my old soccer shirts," I say.

"Good plan," Mom says.

"Hey, everybody," Ben says. "What's the best game to play on Halloween?"

"I don't know, Ben," I say. "Tell me."

"Hide-and-ghost-seek!" he says, laughing.

I smile and shake my head.

On Sunday afternoon, we start working on our costumes. Mine is pretty easy. I've got furry ears, and I'm wearing all black. Dad paints my face with a doggy nose and whiskers, and I even have a furry tail. Dad and I cut up an old Orange Smoothies soccer shirt and make a costume for Bean.

"He's black and orange," I say. "Perfect for Halloween!" It takes the whole family to finish Ben's Halloween costume, which involves about a thousand cotton balls. They keep falling off.

We are just about finished when the doorbell rings. I run to open it, hoping it will be Bella or Josh, but it's Mira, dressed as a wolf. She's with her mom.

"Hi, Mrs. Goldstein," I say.

"Hi, Lola," Mrs. Goldstein says back.

"You look great!" I tell Mira, and she gives me a big growl.

"Very scary," I say. "Come see Ben."

"I'm going to eat him up," Mira says in her best scary voice.

It seems like I'm waiting forever for my friends to come. Every time the doorbell rings, I get excited, but so far it's only been early trick-or-treaters. Josh told me he was coming, but Bella didn't say anything about my pumpkin-gram, so I don't know if she's still mad at me. I'm getting really worried. What if Josh changed his mind? The doorbell rings, and this time, I let my mom answer it.

I hear "Trick or treat!" but I also recognize the voices. It's Bella and Josh, dressed as a fairy and a firefighter. I run to the front door.

"Yay!" I say. "You came!"

"Of course we did," says Bella. "Why wouldn't we?"

"I thought you were mad at me," I tell Bella.

"I was, but only for a little while," she says. "I loved your pumpkin-gram!"

"I'm so glad," I say, and give her a big hug.

"Who are you supposed to be?" asks Josh.

"Bean!" I say, yelling for my puppy. He runs in, and I scoop him up. "And Bean's me. See?"

"I love it!" says Bella, and Josh smiles.

"Does anyone want some hot chocolate before we head out?" Dad asks.

"Yum!" Josh says, and we go into the kitchen.

When we get back from trick-or-treating with Mom and Ms. Benitez, Dad tells all of us to come out into the backyard. We do, and guess what? He has raked all the leaves together into one giant pile.

"Kids," Dad says, "I have a special Halloween gift for you. You can jump and throw and roll around in these leaves, and it will be just fine by me!"

"Yay!" says Ben.

"Really?" asks Mira.

"No way!" says Josh. But I know my dad, so I just wait.

"Is this a trick?" asks Bella.

"No trick," says Dad. "Just a fun Halloween treat."

"Let's go!" I say to Bella and Josh, and then we run and jump and throw leaves. They fly all over the place. *Crunch. Crunch. Crunch.*

"I'm a tree fairy!" yells Bella.

I don't think I've ever had so much fun, not ever. Happy Halloween to us!

Chapter Eight
Strong Bodies

Dear *Diario*,

Well, Halloweek, Halloween, and Halloweekend are all officially over.

I'm not too sad, though, because I have a big soccer tournament this weekend, and we are having extra practices this week. Yay! Ben and I gave up the rest of our Halloween candy. I traded mine for a new pair of shin guards, and Ben traded his for a new book, *101 Jokes for Kids*. Ben sure loves his jokes.

Shalom,
Lola Levine

A few days after Halloween, I give Mom a hug, and she smells like... chocolate.

"Mom!" I say. "Did you keep some of our Halloween candy?"

"Well…," Mom says.

"In this house, we always tell the truth," I say, smiling.

"Yeah, Mom!" says Ben.

"Okay, okay!" Mom says. "I admit it. I did save a few pieces of candy for myself before I threw it out."

"Let's see!" says Ben. Then Mom takes us to her secret candy-hiding place—in the pantry behind the rice.

"Let's get rid of this for good," she says, looking at Dad.

"Dad?!" I say. "Do you have hidden candy, too?"

"I like lollipops" is all he says, and

then he goes out to his studio and comes back with a handful. Ben and I march our parents out to the garbage cans on the curb and *watch* them throw their candy away.

"Good job," I say, patting Mom's back.

"Great idea," Dad says, and Mom agrees.

"Thank you, Lola," Mom says before we go in.

"For what?" I say.

"For reminding me that it's important to take care of my body."

"Strong bodies!" I say, pumping my fist in the air.

"I'm strong!" says Ben, jumping high into the sky.

"Me too!" says Dad, and then he does

a cartwheel on the grass in front of our house. My dad is super silly. "I bet you can't do this!" he tells Mom before doing another cartwheel.

"Oh, yeah?" says Mom. "I bet I can." Then she's cartwheeling on our lawn, too. So, of course, Ben and I have to join in.

"We are the cartwheel family!" says Ben. We all do cartwheels until we are too dizzy and have to stop. Then we lie down on the grass and look up at the clouds in the sky. My family is awesome, in my opinion, and I have lots of opinions!